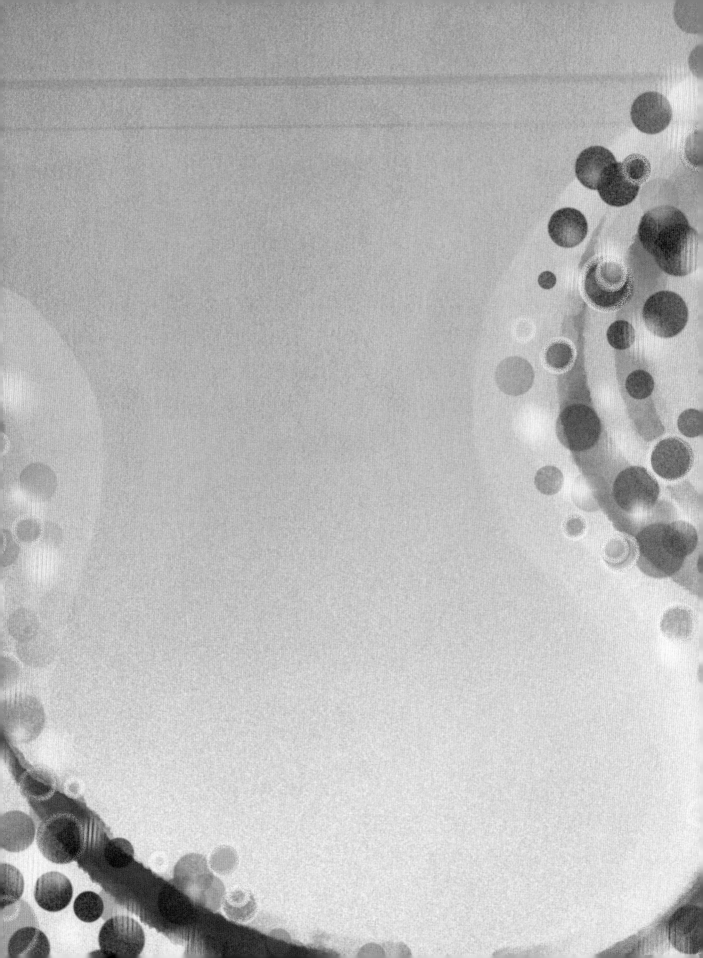

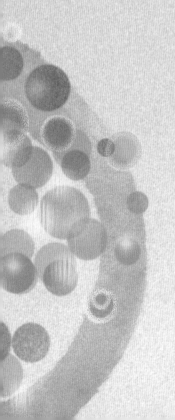

For my daughters, Olivia and Alana,
and for my mom: thank you for making
me the woman I am today.

www.mascotbooks.com

Three Fairies

For more information, please contact:
Mascot Books, an imprint of Amplify Publishing Group
620 Herndon Parkway, Suite 320
Herndon, VA 20170
info@mascotbooks.com

Library of Congress Control Number: 2021917574

CPSIA Code: PRT1221A

ISBN-13: 978-1-64543-983-7

Printed in the United States

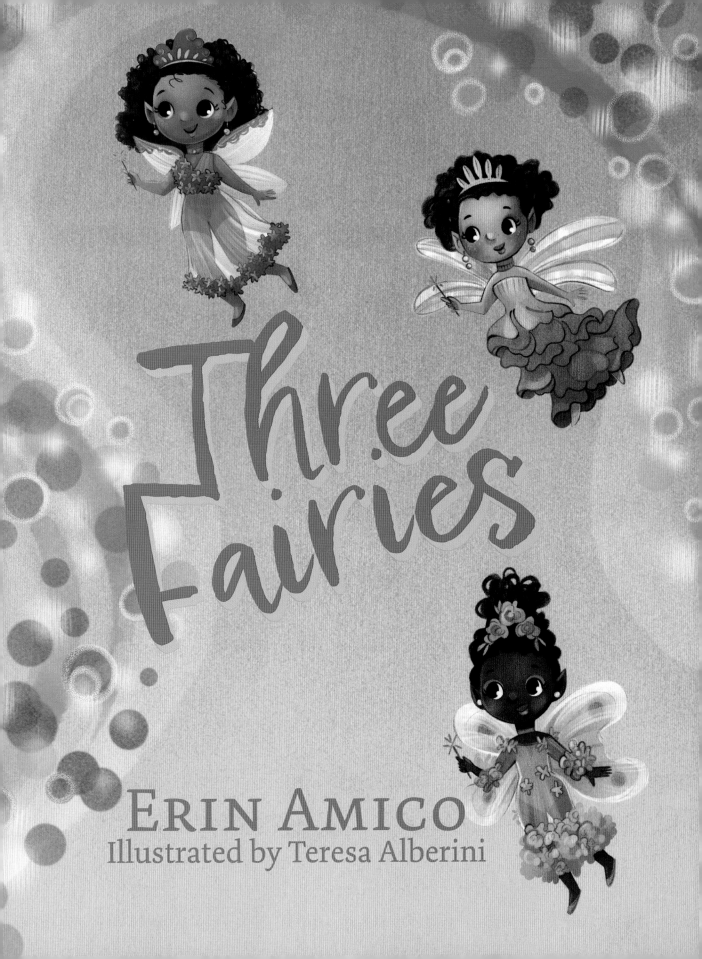

Three Fairies

ERIN AMICO

Illustrated by Teresa Alberini

When the moon was high, and the air was clear,
a mother held her baby girl and whispered three
wishes in her ear.

"My precious girl, as you grow,
there are three things I want you to know.

One: Never change who you truly are.
You're made to shine, just like a star.

Two: Not every smile holds a friend.
Trust your instincts, and never bend.

Three: As you rise and find success,
always remember those who have less.
For even as a tree grows high,
it shares its seeds with the wind for the birds that fly by."

As those words left the mother's lips, they turned to raindrops in long, slow drips.

Those drops then whirled round and round, and with some magic in a blink, the drops turned to fairies: one *blue*, one *violet*, and one *pink*.

Each fairy said hello and then goodbye,
before they rose into the sky.

The years flew by, like a bee from the hive,
and just like that, the baby was five.

She played with blocks at school one day.
(It was her favorite way to play.)

While other kids played Space Cadet,
she said loud and proud, "I'm an architect!"

"Yeah, right," said a girl with a strong dialect.
"Your block tower, I've just wrecked."

Then, without a blink, or a pause, or even a sigh,
a little blue fairy appeared in the sky.

With a smile, she said, "You set the bar.
Never change who you truly are.
You're made to shine, just like a star."

Then the girl said, "Fairy, you are so right.
I'll hold on to my dreams so very tight."

So not in one, or two, but in ten years,
the little girl was building, and building with gears
and wires and stones and big metal beams,
for she had become the architect of her dreams.

With her success came both friend and foe.
One was a man named Billy Bob Joe.

Billy Bob Joe said, "I'll make you a star."
But she knew she just needed herself to go far.
Something wasn't quite right about Billy Bob Joe.
The girl didn't know if he was friend or foe.
Her mind said, *He's tricky,* but his words were so kind,
so she trusted Billy Joe and ignored her mind.

The next day, Billy Joe stole all her supplies.
She sat there, heartbroken, and tears filled her eyes.

Then along came a fairy with a long violet dress,
who said, "My dear girl, don't even stress!
Not every smile holds a friend.
Trust your instincts, and never bend."

"Oh, little fairy," she said, "you set me straight.
I had a feeling that man was not great.
I'll trust my instincts from now on,
and look out for the strangers I come upon."

In a few more years, she turned twenty-five,
and with hard work, her career did thrive.
She became a success and built buildings so high,
some people said they could touch the sky.

One day as she looked out from a building she built,
she noticed a boy in a raggedy kilt.

He had no place to live,
no food and no shelter,
and messy, red hair that was all helter-skelter.

Just as the young lady began to think,
along came a fairy, all dressed in pink.

The fairy said, "As you rise and find success, always remember those who have less.

For even as a tree grows high,
it shares its seeds with the wind for the
birds that fly by."

And with that advice, an idea stirred in the
young lady's head.

She would surprise the boy
by doing what she did best,
for she felt that her life was
really quite blessed.

With metal and glass and
bricks and stones,
she built three fine houses,
three beautiful homes.

She went to the boy with the raggedy kilt,
and said, "I have a present for you. It's something I built."
The boy smiled wide, and his eyes sparked anew,
then he looked at the girl and said warmly, "Thank you."

The young lady turned toward the boy and gave him a wink.
She said, "My friend, I've built you three houses: one *blue*, one *violet*, and one *pink*.

One you must live in, and one you must gift.
The other is for three little fairies, I do insist."

That night, when the moon again rose,
the young boy whispered aloud before his
eyes closed:

One: Never change who you truly are.
You're made to shine, just like a star.

Two: Not every smile holds a friend.
Trust your instincts, and never bend.

Three: As you rise and find success,
always remember those who have less.
For even as a tree grows high,
it shares its seeds with the wind for the
birds that fly by."

About the Author

Erin Amico is a believer in the transformative power of stories. When she's not writing, Erin tells the stories of world-renowned brands in her role as chief marketing officer for a technology-focused nonprofit. She is a Management Leadership for Tomorrow Fellow and has earned master's degrees from Northwestern University and the University of Cambridge.

Erin is inspired by nature, her family, and shedding light on untold stories. She is a poet and author of children's and young adult books. Erin's complete works can be found at ErinAmicoBooks.com.